Dear Parent:

Congratulations! Your child is taking the first steps on an exciting journey. The destination? Independent reading!

STEP INTO READING® will help your child get there. The program offers five steps to reading success. Each step includes fun stories and colorful art. There are also Step into Reading Sticker Books, Step into Reading Math Readers, Step into Reading Write-In Readers, Step into Reading Phonics Readers, and Step into Reading Phonics First Steps! Boxed Sets—a complete literacy program with something for every child.

Learning to Read, Step by Step!

Ready to Read Preschool–Kindergarten
• big type and easy words • rhyme and rhythm • picture clues
For children who know the alphabet and are eager to begin reading.

Reading with Help Preschool–Grade 1
• basic vocabulary • short sentences • simple stories
For children who recognize familiar words and sound out new words with help.

Reading on Your Own Grades 1–3
• engaging characters • easy-to-follow plots • popular topics
For children who are ready to read on their own.

Reading Paragraphs Grades 2–3
• challenging vocabulary • short paragraphs • exciting stories
For newly independent readers who read simple sentences with confidence.

Ready for Chapters Grades 2–4
• chapters • longer paragraphs • full-color art
For children who want to take the plunge into chapter books but still like colorful pictures.

STEP INTO READING® is designed to give every child a successful reading experience. The grade levels are only guides. Children can progress through the steps at their own speed, developing confidence in their reading, no matter what their grade.

Remember, a lifetime love of reading starts with a single step!

www.stepintoreading.com

www.harryandhisbucketfullofdinosaurs.com

Educators and librarians, for a variety of teaching tools, visit us at
www.randomhouse.com/teachers

Library of Congress Cataloging-in-Publication Data
Hooke, R. Schuyler.
Uh-oh! / by R. Schuyler Hooke ; illustrated by Art Mawhinney. — 1st ed.
    p.   cm. — (Step into reading. Step 1)
Based on television program entitled Harry and his bucket full of dinosaurs on Cartoon
Network.
ISBN: 978-0-375-83977-1 (trade) — ISBN: 978-0-375-94056-9 (lib. bdg.)
I. Mawhinney, Art. II. Harry and his bucket full of dinosaurs (Television program). III. Title.
PZ7.H76344Uh 2007   2006027024

Printed in the United States of America
10 9 8 7 6 5   First Edition

Harry and His Bucket Full of Dinosaurs™

Uh-oh!

By R. Schuyler Hooke

Illustrated by Art Mawhinney

Random House 🏠 New York

This is Mom's cup.

Uh-oh!

This <u>was</u> Mom's cup.

What can we do?

Can we hide the cup?

No!

Can we fix the cup?

Yes!

We can fix it
in Dino World!

We need
our bucket!

One . . .

Two . . .

Three . . .

Jump!

I'm on my way
to Dino World!

We need glue!

We have glue!

Taury made
a coffee pot.

Trike made

a bike.

Not a pot! Not a bike!
We must make a cup!

Harry made a cup!

Uh-oh!

It leaks.

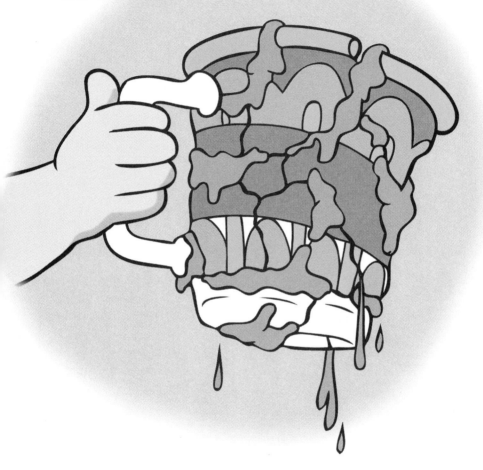

Now we must go home.

Look! Here is my old cup.

We can paint it.
It will be
Mom's new cup.

All done.

Just in time!

Here comes Mom.

I am sorry, Mom.

I broke your cup.

That is okay.

Things can break.

I made you a new cup.

I love my new cup!

You do?

I love my new cup
because you made it.

And I love you.

I love you, too.

Yay!